Mrs Pepperpot at the Bazaar

MRS PEPPERPOT AT THE BAZAAR
A RED FOX BOOK 978 0 099 45158 7

Published in Great Britain by Red Fox,
an imprint of Random House Children's Books

This edition published 2009 for Index Books Ltd

1 3 5 7 9 10 8 6 4 2

Red Fox Books are published by Random House Children's Books,
61–63 Uxbridge Road, London W5 5SA,
a division of The Random House Group Ltd,
in Australia by Random House Australia (Pty) Ltd,
20 Alfred Street, Milsons Point, Sydney, NSW 2061, Australia,
in New Zealand by Random House New Zealand Ltd,
18 Poland Road, Glenfield, Auckland 10, New Zealand,
in South Africa by Random House (Pty) Ltd, Isle of Houghton,
Corner Boundary Road & Carse O'Gowrie, Houghton 2198, South Africa,
and in India by Random House India PVT Ltd, 301 World Trade Tower,
Hotel Intercontinental Grand Complex, Barakhamba Lane, New Delhi 110001, India

THE RANDOM HOUSE GROUP Limited Reg. No. 954009
www.kidsatrandomhouse.co.uk

A CIP catalogue record for this book is available from the British Library.

Printed in China

Mrs Pepperpot at the Bazaar

Alf Prøysen ◉ Hilda Offen

RED FOX

One day Mrs Pepperpot was in her kitchen with her young friend Hannah. Hannah was busy scraping out a bowl and licking the spoon, for the old woman had been making gingerbread shapes.

There was a knock at the door and in walked three very smart ladies.

"Good afternoon," said the smart ladies. "We are collecting prizes for the raffle at the school bazaar. Do you have some little thing we could have?"

"Oh, I'd like to help," said Mrs Pepperpot. "Would a plate of gingerbread be any use?"

"Of course," said the smart ladies.

But as they were leaving they laughed behind her back.

"What a funny old lady and what a silly prize!"

Mrs Pepperpot was very proud and pleased that she was
going to a bazaar.

Hannah was still scraping away at the bowl and licking
the sweet mixture from the spoon. "May I come with you?"
she asked.

"Of course," said Mrs Pepperpot. "Be here at six o'clock."
And she started making another batch of gingerbread shapes.

But when Hannah came back at six the old
woman was not there and she could hear
an odd noise coming from the table.

The mixing bowl was upside down, so she lifted it carefully. And there underneath sat her friend, who was now as small as a pepperpot.

"What a nuisance!" said Mrs Pepperpot. "I was just cleaning out the bowl when I suddenly started shrinking. Then the bowl turned over on me. Quick! Get the gingerbread out of the oven before it burns!"

But it was too late. The gingerbread
was burned to a cinder.

Mrs Pepperpot sat down and cried,
she was so disappointed.

But suddenly she laughed out loud and said, "Hannah! Put me under the tap and give me a good wash. We're going to the bazaar, you and I!"

"But you can't go like that!" said Hannah.

"Oh yes, I can," said Mrs Pepperpot, "as long as you do what I say."

First she asked Hannah to fetch
a silk ribbon and tie it round
her so it looked like a skirt.

Then she told her to fetch some tinsel
from the Christmas decorations.
    Hannah wound it round and round
to make a silver bodice.

And lastly she made a
bonnet of gold foil.

"I've promised them a prize for the bazaar and a prize they must have," said Mrs Pepperpot. "So I'm giving them myself. Just put me down in front of them and say you've brought a clockwork doll. Then pretend to wind me up so that people can see how clever I am."

When Hannah got to the bazaar she put the wonderful doll on the table.

Many people clapped their hands and crowded round to see. "What a pretty doll!" they said. "And what a lovely dress!"

"Look at her golden bonnet!"

Mrs Pepperpot stood completely still and Hannah pretended to wind her up.

Everyone was watching. And when Mrs Pepperpot began to walk across the table there was great excitement.

"Look, the doll can walk!"

And when Mrs Pepperpot began to dance they started shouting with delight, "The doll is dancing!"

The three smart ladies sat in special seats and looked very grand. One of them had given six coffee cups for the raffle, the second a lovely table mat and the third a beautiful iced cake.

They thought the doll was wonderful. Mrs Pepperpot went over to speak to them. The three smart ladies were very pleased.

"Come to me!" said the one who had given the coffee cups.

"Let me hold her a little," said the lady with the table mat.

"Now it's my turn," said the lady with the iced cake.
"Well, I must say, this is a much better prize than
the one that funny old woman offered us today."
Now she should never have said that . . .

Mrs Pepperpot leaped out of her hand and landed PLOP! right in the middle of the beautiful iced cake. Then she waded straight through it. The cake lady screamed, but people were shouting with laughter by now.

"Take that doll away!" shrieked the second lady, but *squish, squash* went Mrs Pepperpot's sticky feet, right across her lovely table mat.

"Get that dreadful doll away from us!" cried the third lady.

But it was too late. Mrs Pepperpot was on the tray with the coffee cups, and began to dance a jig. Cups and saucers flew about and broke in little pieces.

What a to-do!

Suddenly it was time for the raffle.

"First prize will be the wonderful clockwork doll," someone said.

When Hannah heard that, she was very frightened. What would happen if somebody won Mrs Pepperpot?

At last the winning number was called – 311.

Hannah looked at the ticket in her hand. What a piece of luck: it was number 311!

"Hurray!" she cried, and showed her ticket.

So Hannah was allowed to take Mrs Pepperpot home.

Next day the old woman was her proper size again.
   "You're my very own Mrs Pepperpot," said Hannah,
"because I won you at the bazaar."

Discover the wonderful world
of MRS PEPPERPOT with
these lively picture books:

Mrs Pepperpot Learns to Swim
Mrs Pepperpot Minds the Baby
Mrs Pepperpot and the Treasure
Mrs Pepperpot at the Bazaar

And our bestselling fiction title
for older readers:

Mrs Pepperpot Stories

Life is never dull
with the irrepressible
MRS PEPPERPOT!